GO DIEGO GO!

ANIMAL RESCUER

Science

Photo page 9 top © Michael Melford/The Image Bank/Getty Images
Photo page 9 bottom © Amos Nachoum/The Image Bank/Getty Images

Published by Scholastic Inc., 90 Old Sherman Turnpike, Danbury, CT 06816

SCHOLASTIC and associated logos are trademarks and/or registered trademarks of Scholastic Inc.

ISBN 0-439-90706-3

Printed in the U.S.A.

First Scholastic Printing, February 2007

Watching the Whales

by
Sarah Albee

illustrated by
Warner McGee

SCHOLASTIC INC.

New York Toronto London Auckland Sydney
Mexico City New Delhi Hong Kong Buenos Aires

"I hear an animal in trouble that needs our help!" said Diego. He and his sister, Alicia, were working at the Animal Rescue Center.

"Our special camera, Click, can help us find the animal in trouble," said Alicia.

Click zoomed to the ocean and found the animal who was calling for help. "It's a baby humpback whale," Diego said. "But what's wrong?"

"We're going to need to find out more about humpback whales so we can help him," Diego said.

Alicia downloaded information about the humpback whale on the Science Deck computer.

"Humpback whales are called 'acrobats of the sea' because they are excellent swimmers. They swim in groups called pods," Alicia read.

Breaching

Mother with Baby

"Oh no!" cried Diego. "The baby humpback whale that Click found is not with his pod. We need to rescue him! *¡Al rescate!*"

Diego and Alicia quickly made their way to the beach.

"How will we get all the way to the baby humpback whale?" Alicia wondered.

"Rescue Pack can help," said Diego. *"¡Actívate!"*

Immediately Rescue Pack changed into a speedboat.

Diego and Alicia sprang into the boat. They zoomed off in the direction of Baby Humpback Whale.

"Diego, Alicia! I'm so glad you're here!" called Baby Humpback Whale, when Diego and Alicia arrived.

12

"I got separated from my mommy and the other whales when a noisy ship passed by me. Will you help me find my pod again?"

"No problem," said Diego. "Maybe I can spot them using my binoculars."

14

While Diego looked, Baby Humpback Whale poked his head and upper body high out of the water. "If I do this, I can look, too," he said.

"That's called spy hopping!" Alicia told Diego. But they saw no sign of the pod.

"Maybe we could send them a signal somehow," Diego suggested.

"Good idea!" replied Baby Humpback Whale. He leaped out of the water, spinning his shining body around as he did so.

"Wow!" said Alicia. "Look how high he can jump!"
"That's called breaching," Diego said. "Whales do that to tell each other where they are."

The pod was still nowhere to be seen. But as he scanned the horizon, Diego noticed three pointy, gray fins zooming toward them through the water!

"Uh-oh!" said Diego, pointing.

"Sharks!" exclaimed Alicia. "We need to get away from here—fast!"

"Wait, I know something that might scare them away," said Baby Humpback Whale. "I'm going to try lob tailing. Hang on tight!"

Baby Humpback Whale plunged his head downward, then stuck his tail out of the water. His tail slapped the water as it swung back and forth. *Wham! Wham! Wham!*

Diego and Alicia hung on to the rescue boat as it bounced up and down on the waves.

"Look, Alicia!" Diego shouted. "The sharks are swimming away! Great lob tailing, Baby Humpback Whale!"

"Thanks, Diego. I just wish I could find my mommy so I could tell her about scaring away the sharks," Baby Humpback Whale said.

"Don't worry, we'll find her," Diego assured him. "Why don't you try calling to your pod under the water?"

"Yes! I can send a sound signal through the water," said Baby Humpback Whale. "I'll be right back." He dove beneath the surface.

Diego and Alicia lowered an underwater microphone into the water so that they could hear Baby Humpback Whale singing. And a moment later they heard the pod singing back!

Baby Humpback Whale leaped high into the air, slapping his tail against the water as he came back down. "I heard them! They're coming!" he said excitedly.

Moments later the pod of whales came zooming toward them, breaching through the waves.

"I see my mommy!" called Baby Humpback Whale to
Diego and Alicia. As he quickly swam over to Mommy
Humpback Whale, he called out, *"¡Gracias, amigos!"*
  The two whales leaped and spun playfully in the water
as they swam away.

"No wonder they're called 'acrobats of the sea,'" laughed Diego, as he and Alicia watched the pod of whales leap through the waves. "*¡Misión cumplida!* Rescue complete!"

Nick Jr. Play-to-Learn™ Fundamentals
Skills every child needs, in stories every child will love!

 colors + shapes — Recognizing and identifying basic shapes and colors in the context of a story.

 emotions — Learning to identify and understand a wide range of emotions, such as happy, sad, and excited.

 imagination — Fostering creative thinking skills through role-play and make-believe.

123 math — Recognizing early math in the world around us, such as patterns, shapes, numbers, and sequences.

music + movement — Celebrating the sounds and rhythms of music and dance.

physical — Building coordination and confidence through physical activity and play.

problem solving — Using critical thinking skills, such as observing, listening, and following directions, to make predictions and solve problems.

reading + language — Developing a lifelong love of reading through high interest stories and characters.

science — Fostering curiosity and an interest in the natural world around us.

social skills + cultural diversity — Developing respect for others as unique, interesting people.

Science

Conversation Spark

*Questions and activities for
play-to-learn parenting.*

Whales can leap, spin, dive,
and even sing! Try
moving like the whales
in this story.

For more parent and kid-friendly
activities, go to www.nickjr.com.

ENGLISH/SPANISH GLOSSARY
and PRONUNCIATION GUIDE

ENGLISH	SPANISH	PRONUNCIATION
To the rescue	Al rescate	al res-CAH-teh
Activate	Actívate	ahk-TEE-vah-tay
Thank you	Gracias	GRAH-see-ahs
Friends	Amigos	ah-MEE-gohs
Rescue	Misión	mee-see-OHN
Complete	Cumplida	coom-PLEE-dah